E
Rad

1036725

W9-BKN-583

Molly

by Ruth Shaw Radlauer

illustrated by Emily Arnold McCully

Prentice-Hall Books for Young Readers

A Division of Simon & Schuster, Inc., New York

Published by Prentice-Hall Books for Young Readers
A Division of Simon & Schuster, Inc.
Simon & Schuster Building, Rockefeller Center
1230 Avenue of the Americas, New York, NY 10020

10 9 8 7 6 5 4 3 2 1

Prentice-Hall Books for Young Readers
is a trademark of Simon & Schuster, Inc.
Printed in Spain
This book is a work of fiction. Names, characters,
places and incidents are either the product of the
author's imagination or are used fictitiously.
Any resemblance to actual events or locales or
persons, living or dead, is entirely coincidental.

Library of Congress Cataloging-in-Publication Data
Radlauer, Ruth Shaw, 1926-
Molly.
Summary: Molly, a rambunctious four-year-old,
has a busy day at nursery school painting, playing,
pasting, and tricycle riding.
[1. Nursery schools—Fiction.   2. Schools—
Fiction]   I. McCully, Emily Arnold, ill.   II. Title.
PZ7.R122Mnr 1986   [E]   86-22566
ISBN 0-13-599762-3

To the child within me, Frances Ruth

"Molly! Comb your hair."

"Molly! Pull up your socks."

"Molly! Wash your face."

"Molly! Tuck in your blouse."

"Leave Mr. Bear on your bed

and zip up your jacket."

"There now, Molly.
    You're all ready for school."

Molly went to school.

She played with blocks…

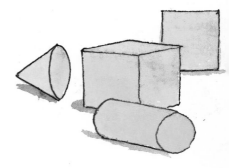

and painted a picture.
She liked the blue paint best!

Molly rode the tricycle

and learned a new song.

Then she listened to a story about a clown

and pasted a paper clown together.

Molly rode home from school.

"Oh, Molly!"

"What?"

"Oh—well—I see you had
a wonderful day at school."